Junkyard Dan

Plans

NOX PRESS
books for that extra kick to give you more power
www.NoxPress.com

Also by Elise Leonard:

The **JUNKYARD DAN** series: (***Nox Press***)

1. Start of a New Dan
2. Dried Blood
3. Stolen?
4. Gun in the Back
5. Plans
6. Money for Nothing
7. Stuffed Animal
8. Poison, Anyone?
9. A Picture Tells a Thousand Dollars
10. Wrapped Up
11. Finished
12. Bloody Knife
13. Taking Names and Kicking Assets
14. Mercy

THE SMITH BROTHERS (a series): (***Nox Press***)

1. All for One
2. When in Rome
3. Get a Clue
4. The Hard Way
5. Master Plan

A LEEG OF HIS OWN (a series): (***Nox Press***)

1. Croaking Bullfrogs, Hidden Robbers
2. 20,000 LEEGS Under the C
3. Failure to Lunch
4. Hamlette

The **AL'S WORLD** series: (***Simon & Schuster***)

Book 1: Monday Morning Blitz
Book 2: Killer Lunch Lady
Book 3: Scared Stiff
Book 4: Monkey Business

The **LEADER** series: (***Nox Press***)

✮ Honor
✮ Courage
✮ Respect
✮ Service
✮ Integrity
✮ Commitment
✮ Loyalty
✮ Duty

Junkyard Dan

Plans

Elise Leonard

books for that extra kick to give you more power
www.NoxPress.com

Leonard, Elise
Junkyard Dan series / Plans
ISBN: 978-0-9815694-4-4

Copyright © 2008 by Elise Leonard.
All rights reserved, including the right of reproduction in whole or in part in any form. Published by Nox Press.
www.NoxPress.com

First Nox Press printing: June 2008
Second Nox Press printing: March 2009
Third Nox Press printing: April 2010

books for that extra kick to give you more power

This book is dedicated to all who have sacrificed
in the defense of freedom, equality, human dignity
and all things that lift ***all*** people to a higher
and better place.
For those who sincerely support literacy
and for those who are working to obtain it,
I salute you!

Nox Press would like to recognize the Executive
Director of the New Mexico Coalition for
Literacy, Heather Heunermund.
Heather is a shining example of what an
executive director should be.
She cares about the people she serves,
ever mindful to the needs of others.
Her hard work, empathy and compassion should
be an example not only to every literacy program
director, but to every executive director (in *any*
capacity), every educator and every human being.
Nox Press would like to acknowledge and thank
Heather Heunermund for caring so deeply.

Special thanks to Rafael Soto (AKA: Billy the Kid)
for letting us use his cool truck on the cover!
And thanks, again, to the guys at TC Autoworks in
Donna, Texas, who custom painted Rafael's truck.
[The truck is called "The Outlaw."]

~Elise

Chapter 1

It had been a few days since I'd found out. Found out about the machine gun.

I hadn't returned it to the sheriff yet.

I'd wanted a little time to myself. To relax.

Hadn't had much of that lately.

It seemed I went from one thing to the next.

But not these last couple of days. These last couple days? I worked at doing nothing.

It was harder than I'd thought.

I kept coming up with stuff to do. But then I'd stop.

I'd tell myself that I had to do nothing.

That it was time to relax.

So there I was. Sitting in my office. Surfing the

Internet. Just playing.

That's when Bubba drove up.

He barreled through my office door.

"So how have you been?" he asked.

"Great," I said. I grinned.

"Have you gotten your R&R?" he asked.

I smiled. "Sure have."

"So what did you do?" he asked.

I wasn't used to this.

Small-town living.

People asked so many questions.

I wasn't used to that.

An entire *town* knew my business.

I wasn't used to that, either.

But I'd better *get* used to it. Because that's how my life was now.

Not that I minded. Not really.

I kind of liked it. People cared.

At least the people in Peaceville did.

In New York? No one cared.

I'd left New York.

Just got up and walked away. And I've yet to

Plans

receive one call or letter.

No one asked where I was.

No one noticed that I was gone.

I'd dropped off the face of the Earth. And no one cared.

That was New York.

But in Peaceville? If I spent too long in the *bathroom*? I had to explain myself to at *least* two people.

Bubba. And Hilda. And possibly Judge Simpkins. But he wasn't as bad as Bubba or Hilda.

And I had to explain myself to a whole *bunch* of animals. Mostly cats and dogs.

I have many.

How many?

I couldn't give you a head count!

But they're mine. And I have to take care of them.

"So?" Bubba asked. "What *did* you do with your time off?"

"Just had a little down time," I told him. "I didn't do much. Not much of anything, really."

Bubba nodded. "Good. That's what you wanted."

"Yes," I said.

Bubba looked around. "So. Are you ready to get back to things?" he asked.

For now? I'd done enough "nothing" to last me a while. "Yes, I think so," I said.

Bubba grinned. "Good. Because I brought you the machine gun."

"Okay," I said. "I'll bring it to the sheriff."

"When?" he asked.

I shrugged. "Some time today."

Bubba nodded. "Okay. What about those plans?" he asked.

I knew what he was speaking about.

While I was gone? He sold a door to someone. It was from a 1991 Chevy pickup.

When Bubba took off the door? Some plans fell out.

They were hidden in the door.

Between the metal outside and the inside.

"They're probably nothing," I said.

Plans

Bubba looked nervous.

That wasn't good.

Bubba was a laid-back type of guy. If he looked nervous? It *couldn't* be good.

I had a sinking feeling. Right in the pit of my stomach.

"Okay," I said. "Spill it."

"Well," Bubba started off slowly. "While you were off? Taking some time to relax? I looked over those papers. The ones from the door."

"And?" I asked.

"Well," he said slowly. He was trying to gauge my reaction. "Don't go off the deep end…"

I looked at him. Waited for it.

"Just tell me, okay?" I said with a long sigh.

"Well. You know how you just said that they're probably nothing?"

"Yes?" I said slowly. Not wanting to hear the answer.

"They're not 'nothing.' Someone told me that they're important."

That's what I was afraid of.

Chapter 2

"Before I start on the *next* problem? Can I at *least* wrap up the *last* one?!" I said in a huff.

Bubba laughed.

"Sure thing, Dan." His grin was wide. "Don't get your panties in a wad."

"They're *not* in a wad," I said loudly.

Bubba cracked up.

Then he winked at me. As if he were saying, "Got ya!"

"And I *don't* wear *panties*!" I added.

I added that for good measure. But it only made Bubba laugh louder.

He shook his head. His chuckles dying in his throat.

Plans

"It's just too easy with you, Dan," he said.

I shot him a look.

"You *really* need to lighten up," he said.

What Bubba *didn't* realize? This *was* the "lighter" version of me!

"If you don't lighten up," Bubba started. Then he shook his head.

"What?" I asked.

"That surgery is going to be painful!" he replied.

I looked at him. Closely.

"What surgery?" I asked.

I thought of a heart attack.

Open heart surgery.

I thought of a stroke.

Brain surgery.

I thought of other scary surgeries.

Surgeries brought on by stress.

Bubba smiled widely. "The surgery to remove that stick from your—"

"Okay. Okay. I get it," I said before he could finish his sentence.

I didn't take offense. I *should* have. But I didn't.

Bubba didn't mean any harm.

It was the opposite.

He wanted to help. Wanted me to lighten up.

He made a good point. Not about the stick up my, ah, well, you know. But about how I needed to chill out. Relax.

To be honest? I'd worked so hard trying to relax? I bet I really didn't get *that* much rest.

But, like the saying went. There's not much rest for the weary.

And I was one of them. You know. The "weary."

It seemed there was always something.

Something I had to do.

Something I had to fix.

Something I had to find out.

Some problem I had to solve.

Like now. With those plans.

"So where are the plans now?" I asked Bubba.

"At the library. Henry Pake has them."

Plans

"Why?" I asked.

"He's in the reserves. I figured he could help," Bubba explained.

That made sense.

I nodded. "Okay."

"You'll have to go there. To get the plans," Bubba said.

See? I had to go to the sheriff's office. And now? I had to go to the library too!

"I'll go to the sheriff's first," I said aloud.

I wasn't talking to Bubba. Just to myself. Out loud.

Planning my day.

Bubba nodded. Like he was giving his approval.

I shot him a look.

"If you don't mind, that is," I said.

He grinned back at me.

"Nah," he said. "I don't mind. Sure. Hit the sheriff's first."

I rolled my eyes.

Either Bubba didn't *sense* that I was trying to

bust his chops. Or Bubba didn't care.

I think he didn't care.

I held out my hand. "I'll take that."

Bubba placed the machine gun in my open palm.

"Goodbye, my friend," Bubba said. "You will be missed."

I tried not to smile.

"Don't worry, Bubba. I'll be back," I replied. "The sheriff will know it's not my gun."

Bubba laughed loudly.

"I wasn't talking to *you*! I was talking to the gun," he said.

I just stared at him.

"It kind of grew on me," he explained.

"Bill McCoy's Tommy gun?"

"Yeah," he said. "It's a piece of history."

Chapter 3

The long drive? To the sheriff's office? It was odd!

Why was it odd?

It was just weird. You know. Having a machine gun.

That was new to me.

What was even weirder? Having it on the seat. Right there. Next to me.

Before I got to the car? I tried to put it in a bag.

A plastic bag. From the grocery store.

That didn't work out.

One, it wouldn't fit. The gun was too big.

And two, it ripped the bag.

The gun was too heavy.

Plus, it would have been "concealed."

You know. A concealed weapon.

That wouldn't be good.

I didn't want to drive around with a concealed weapon.

So I just sat it there. On the seat. Next to me.

Out in the open. Not concealed.

Of course, I stayed at speed limit.

I didn't want to get stopped. Or pulled over.

That's all I needed.

To get pulled over. *And* to have a machine gun at my side.

I'd probably get arrested.

I thought of the news. And the headlines that would follow.

MAN FOUND WITH MACHINE GUN.

DAN CORBETT. HE *USED* TO BE A NICE GUY!

Then I thought of Patti reading it. Patti being my almost ex-wife. (We aren't divorced yet. I'm still waiting for her to make the first move on that.)

Plans

Anyhow. The thought of Patti reading that article? It made me smile.

Well, not Patti reading it. *Neil* reading it.

The thought of Neil reading it? *That* made me smile.

Neil is the 23-year-old roofer Patti ran off with.

I smiled at the thought. I could picture Neil reading such a news story.

Or *seeing* it!

Oh, yes. That would be better!

I thought of my face. Plastered on the TV.

Me. A tough guy! A "man with a machine gun."

Just like Bill McCoy.

But I was like Bill McCoy in another way, too.

I'd never hurt anyone.

Not on purpose.

But I'd want Neil to think I could. Possibly. Maybe.

Even for just a split second.

Not that I'd ever *do* anything to hurt him. But Neil didn't know that.

And for that one split second? When he got scared? *That* would be payback.

Payback for all the pain he'd caused me. Forced me to go through.

And the anguish.

Chapter 4

I got to the sheriff's office. No problem.

No one pulled me over.

No one stopped me.

No police officers.

No people.

No hassles.

No sweat. (Okay. Maybe a little sweat. *My* sweat.)

But in the end? No one even knew about the gun.

Oh well. I guess Neil would just have to live with his conscience.

But something told me? He didn't care how I was feeling.

If he *did*? He wouldn't have run off with my wife.

He probably didn't *have* a conscience, either.

If he *did*? He wouldn't have run off with my wife!

I walked into the sheriff's office.

It looked like I thought it would look.

Old. Shabby.

Stuffy.

There was only one person there. A young guy.

A deputy.

He was sitting behind the front desk.

"May I help you?" he asked me.

I held out the gun.

Before I could blink? He had his revolver out. And it was cocked and aimed.

Right at me.

Hm. That was twice now. This was the *second* time!

Before I owned the junkyard? I'd *never* had anyone point a gun at me. Ever!

Now? In a short time? *Two* people had pointed

Plans

guns at me.

"Whoa," I said calmly. "Slow down there."

I slowly moved the machine gun. Very slowly.

Inch by inch.

No quick movements. Nothing fancy.

I placed it on the counter.

Eased it onto the counter.

The deputy's hand started to shake.

"Stay calm, man," I said softly.

I could see sweat beading on his upper lip.

"It's okay," I said. "I'm returning this to you."

I tried not to move. Tried to show him I was not a danger to him.

I raised my hands slowly.

Just then the sheriff came bursting through the door. The door I just came through.

He was holding a box of donuts.

When he saw his deputy's gun trained on me? He dropped those donuts. Then he tore out his weapon, too.

Great. Now I had *three* people pull guns on me.

But at the moment I was only thinking of the

last two.

The one in front of me.

And the one behind me.

Both excellent shots. (I'm sure.) And both trained to kill.

"I'm Dan Corbett," I said quickly.

My hands were still above my head.

"I'm here to return Bill McCoy's machine gun," I added. Also quickly.

I wouldn't want a stray bullet to go off before I could explain.

Chapter 5

"Hi Dan," the sheriff said. "Nice to finally meet you. I've heard nice things about you. From Bubba."

He was still squatting. His gun still aimed at my chest.

Then it must have hit him. Because he smiled.

He also holstered his gun.

His eyes flew to the donuts on the floor.

"Dang it!" he said. "I was really looking forward to those."

Then he looked at his deputy.

"What the heck are you *doing*?!" he bellowed.

The young deputy wilted.

"I'm sorry, Sheriff. He had a gun. I just…

reacted."

The sheriff shook his head and tsked.

Tsk. Tsk. Tsk. "Haven't you seen *Men in Black*?!" the sheriff said with annoyance.

The deputy nodded. "Yes, sir."

"And what did it *teach* you?!" the sheriff roared.

The deputy looked confused.

He shrugged.

"That aliens are all around us?" he croaked weakly.

He didn't look too sure of his answer.

And with *that* answer, he *shouldn't* have!

I think I knew what the sheriff was getting at.

"You mean the scene where Will Smith shoots the little girl with the Calculus books?" I asked.

"That's right, Dan!" the sheriff said.

He came over to me and clapped me on my back.

Then he shook my hand and smiled.

"You need to judge things. On the spot," he said to his deputy. "Anyone can see this man is

Plans

not here for trouble!"

What did he mean by *that*?!

Did I look that pathetic?

I hoped not.

The sheriff turned back to me.

"So," he said as he looked at the machine gun. "This was Bill McCoy's gun?"

He picked it up to look closer.

"Yes," I said.

"Cool," he said with a grin.

"So I can just leave it here with you?" I asked.

"Sure," the sheriff said.

"It should go into a museum," the deputy said.

You know? He was right. "That's a good idea," I said.

The sheriff laughed. "Every now and then? He has a good idea."

The deputy looked a little hurt.

"That's why I keep him around," the sheriff added.

Then he laughed.

"He's a little green," the sheriff said about the

deputy. "And his reactions are a little off. But his instincts are good."

The young deputy now looked pleased.

"With a little work? He'll be a good law officer," the sheriff stated proudly.

The deputy was beaming.

"Thanks, boss," he said.

The sheriff waved off his comment. "Don't let it go to your head, son."

The sheriff walked me to the door.

"So where are you heading now?" the sheriff asked me.

"To the library. To speak with the librarian about something," I said as we reached the door.

"You mean about those plans?" he asked.

I was surprised.

"How'd you know about them?" I asked him.

"Bubba told me."

I rolled my eyes and sighed loudly.

Yup. I had to get used to small-town living.

Chapter 6

I drove to the library next. It was a beautiful building.

New.

It had lots of glass. And looked modern.

And it was very quiet inside.

My mom had taken me to the library a *lot* when I was a kid.

I loved the library.

I could spend the whole day there. Looking at pictures of dinosaurs. And trucks.

It was a special place for me. Magical.

But then I grew older.

And, sadly, the library lost its magic.

I think it was due to the mean librarian we'd

had at the time.

She was *so* mean.

It was hard to forget her.

Mrs. Ingram.

She would shush *anyone*! For *anything*!

There was an old man there once. When I was in sixth grade. I'll never forget.

The man was choking.

Sounded like he was about to cough up a lung or something.

And did that old biddy do anything to help him?

No.

She *shushed* him!

Can you believe it?!

He was about to cough up a lung. I was afraid he was going to die!

And she *shushed* him.

She gave librarians a bad rep.

Because ever since Mrs. Ingram? I've yet to meet a librarian I didn't like.

Most of them were nice. And helpful.

Plans

They actually *liked* to see people in their libraries.

But Mrs. Ingram? You'd swear she hated people. Especially kids.

Maybe she liked books. But she didn't like people.

I was lost in thoughts of grumpy old Mrs. Ingram.

I walked quietly across the carpet.

I didn't see the man sitting in the hallway until I plowed into him.

Anyone else? I would have knocked down.

But this guy? He was *huge*! He didn't budge.

"I'm so sorry," I said right away. "I didn't see you sitting there."

"I didn't hear you come in," he said. "That's why I sit here. To listen for patrons."

He started rolling up some… yarn. Into a ball.

"I was trying to be quiet," I told him. "I didn't want to get shushed."

His tough face softened as he smiled. "I'm not the shushing type of librarian."

"Thank goodness," I said. "I bet the kids like you."

He grimaced. "I think they're a little afraid of me, at first."

"Oh," I said. I didn't know what else to say to him.

"Well, I *am* a huge, bald, tough-looking black man," he said with a grin.

"Hey." I threw my hands in the air. "I didn't say that."

He laughed. "No. But you probably thought it."

"You *are* a big man. What are you? About two fifty? Two sixty?" I asked.

"Two eighty," he said. But then he looked shy. "But that's only because muscle weighs more than fat."

This was a very strange chat.

He must have sensed me thinking that.

"I used to be a chubby kid. The other kids were cruel," he explained.

I nodded. "I wasn't one of the cool kids either," I told him.

Plans

It was his turn to nod.

"We probably would have been friends," I said with a smile.

He agreed.

I looked down at his hands.

He was holding a tiny little pink… sweater.

Too big for a doll, but *way* too small for him.

I didn't say anything. But I sure was curious.

"Oh. Sorry," he said. "I was focused on my work."

His work?

"I didn't want to lose a stitch," he said.

If it were anyone else? I would have made a crack.

You know, something like: "I hate when that happens."

But like the man said. He *was* a huge, bald, tough-looking black man.

I didn't think he'd like my crack. So I said nothing.

"I'm Henry. The town librarian," he said.

"I'm Dan. Dan Corbett. Junkyard Dan."

Chapter 7

"Hey. It's great to finally meet you," he said. "Bubba talks about you all the time."

I smiled. "Maybe you should shush him."

He laughed. A deep rumbling laugh. "You can't shush Bubba. That just makes him talk more. For spite."

I had to laugh at that.

Mostly because it was true.

"Come on with me," he said.

I followed him to his office.

His computer screen had a picture of dog on it. And there were framed photos of the same dog on his desk. His very large desk.

I guess a man of his size needed a large desk.

Plans

I noticed the dog wearing a sweater in one of the photos.

"Oh," I said aloud. "It's a sweater. For your *dog*!"

That got Henry laughing.

"Who did you think it was for? Me?" he asked.

I shrugged and smiled. "I had no clue."

"That's Peggy Sue. She's my basset hound."

"She's cute," I said. And she *was* cute.

"I make this special design sweater. It has pockets. To hold her ears. They drag down to the ground."

He held up his sweater and poked his finger into a pocket. The he poked his finger into another pocket.

"I tuck her ears in here so they don't drag in the snow," he explained.

That got me confused. We were in Florida. "Snow?" I asked.

"I go home to visit my folks. Every year. For Christmas. They live in upstate New York. Poor Peggy Sue freezes her buns off."

"Ah," I said.

"I used to have another dog. Lucille. She was a bagel," he said.

"A bagel?"

"A basset hound and a beagle. A bagel."

That made me laugh.

"She was old. But I *still* think she wasn't used to the cold. She died when I was visiting my folks. So ever since, I make Peggy Sue wear a sweater."

That made sense.

"And the pockets are great for her ears," I noted.

His smile was huge. "That's right."

He put the sweater on his desk. Then he opened a drawer and took out the plans. The plans Bubba found in the door.

He smoothed them out on the desk.

"The truck was a 1991. Do you think the plans are from Desert Storm?" I asked.

Henry shook his head. "I wish."

"They're military plans. Right?" I asked.

"Right," he said.

Plans

"From a war zone?" I guessed.

"Yes."

"But not from Desert Storm?" I asked.

"No," he said.

I hated to ask. "From what war?"

He looked upset.

Chapter 8

"I was in the reserves," Henry said.

I listened quietly.

"We got called up," he added.

I nodded.

"We stayed there for years," he said softly. "Too many years."

He grabbed for his knitting.

"I'm sorry," he said. "It relaxes me."

"I understand," I said. "I wish *I* had something that relaxed me."

Henry turned in his chair. He opened a drawer and took out a ball of yarn. And two knitting needles.

He handed them to me.

Plans

"I don't knit," I said.

"I'll teach you," he replied.

He grabbed another ball of yarn. And two more needles.

"I'll start a new project so we can do the same thing," he said.

Then he showed me what to do.

I was all thumbs.

I couldn't do it.

At least, not well.

"What stitch is this?" I asked Henry.

"A knit stitch."

I nodded. "What are we making?" I asked.

"A scarf."

"But this is Florida," I said with a smile.

He smiled back. "With all those holes? You're not going to have to worry about being too warm."

I smiled. "Good point."

He showed me a different stitch.

I had trouble with that one too.

It looked bad. Worse than the other stitch.

My scarf looked pitiful. It looked like Swiss

cheese.

"What's *this* stitch called?" I asked.

"A purl," he said.

"A *pearl*?" I asked. "Like a diamond?"

"No. P U R L," he spelled out. "Purl."

"Oh," I said.

Even the stitch names were girlie.

Henry had this weird way of knowing what I was thinking.

"What do you *want* it to be called?" he asked. "A touchdown? A dunk? A run? A lap?"

I held up my "scarf."

"This looks like a 'run,'" I said with a crooked smile.

It looked like Patti's stockings.

When they had a run in them? They looked like this.

A heap. A big mixed-up tangle.

My scarf looked pathetic.

"You'll get it in time," Henry said. "If you keep with it."

"I don't know if this is my thing," I said

Plans

truthfully.

Henry looked at my scarf. "Yeah. Probably not."

I put down my needles.

"When did you start knitting?" I asked Henry.

"A long time ago. When I was younger. Long before I was shipped out."

I nodded.

"I knitted all through my tours in Iraq. It was a horrible place."

"Did the guys tease you?" I asked.

He raised his eyebrows. "Would you?"

I looked at the large man. "No."

"Neither did they," he said.

Then he laughed.

"They may have *thought* things," he said. "But they never *said* anything. Not a word."

"I'm sure not," I said with a chuckle.

"My biker friends don't say anything either," Henry said.

Oh, yes. That's right. I'd heard rumors.

Our town librarian was a biker dude.

A biker dude who knits when he's stressed.

A biker dude who knits sweaters for his dog. His basset hound.

His dog named Peggy Sue.

I looked at the photos again.

She really was cute.

"Your plans are from Iraq," Henry blurted out.

"From 1991?" I asked.

He put down his knitting. He looked me head on.

His face was tough.

His eyes were hard. Steely.

"No. They're recent," he said.

Chapter 9

Henry could be a very scary guy.

He was so intense.

"Sorry," he said. "Your plans brought back bad memories."

His hands were moving quickly.

"Iraq was…" He looked up from his knitting.

I could see pain on his face.

"Iraq was one of the hardest things I've ever done," he said.

He went back to knitting.

"I saw things," he said.

His fingers were moving quickly.

"Horrible things."

I felt for him. Not just for him. But for all of

our men and women in the service.

"Things a human being shouldn't see."

I didn't know what to say to him.

He pointed his chin at the plans.

"That's a map," he said.

"A map?" I asked.

He nodded. "Of a bad place."

"You know where it is?" I asked.

"Yes."

"You can tell just by looking at that?" I asked.

I pictured the "plans" in my mind.

It had looked like a treasure map to me. Nothing marked. No street names.

Just a big, hand-drawn thing.

It had lots of Xs and arrows. Lots of strange symbols. They looked primitive. Or like you had to know the secret. The secret to what they meant.

I didn't have a clue.

I didn't know the secret.

But Henry did.

It didn't look like anything scary to me.

But whatever it was? It was scary to Henry.

Plans

Which was weird.

You wouldn't think *anything* could scare a big man like Henry.

"I've been there," he repeated. "I hope I never go back there."

"Where?" I asked.

"Iraq."

I walked to the plans. I looked at them.

It didn't look like Iraq to me.

It could have been anywhere.

Boise, Idaho.

San Diego, California.

New York, New York.

For all I knew? It could have been Peaceville, Florida!

"How do you know it's Iraq?" I asked Henry.

"I just do," he said.

"And you've been there?" I pointed to the treasure map.

"Sure have."

"At that exact place?" I asked.

I looked closely. Next to all the Xs and the

other strange markings was a star.

Not like a Christmas star.

Someone had hand written an **X**. Then they put a plus sign on top. (**+**)

"What are all the Xs?" I asked.

Henry was knitting like mad now.

"Land mines."

Oh. Wow. "What are all the squiggle things?"

"Booby traps."

"What do the hand-shaded regions mean?" I asked.

"A sniper can pick you off easily in those areas."

I think I went pale.

"Are you okay?" Henry asked me.

I nodded. "That didn't…" My voice cracked.

I cleared my throat. I tried to speak again.

I looked at the map again.

"That didn't leave much safe space," I croaked out.

Henry shook his head. "Nope. It sure didn't."

Plans

"What's this star?" I asked.

Henry shrugged. "I don't know."

I brought him the map. So he could see.

"Here," I said. I pointed to that **X** with the **+** on top. "What is this?"

"I have no idea," Henry said simply.

"Someone wrote it," I said.

Henry smiled. "You think?" he cracked at me.

I grinned at him. "Well, if someone wrote it? It must mean *something*."

"I'm sure it does," Henry said.

"But you don't know what it means."

Henry grinned. "Nope."

I stood there thinking.

"Whose car did it come from?" Henry asked.

"I don't know. It was a truck. I'll have to trace the VIN number."

"Your answer might be there," he offered.

He was right.

Chapter 10

I stopped at the town garage.

Bubba was fixing an old car.

"Hi," I said loudly.

Bubba stood up. He banged his head on the car's hood. "Ow!"

I had to laugh.

"Do that often?" I asked him.

"I'd think that once was too often. Wouldn't you?" he cracked.

He rubbed his head.

"I just got back from the library," I said.

"And?"

"And Henry said those plans are from Iraq."

Bubba nodded.

Plans

"If anyone would know, it's him," Bubba said. "Henry served a couple tours."

I nodded. "It seems he's still trying to get over it."

Bubba shrugged. "He may never. He saw a lot."

Once again, I felt sorry for Henry. "That's what he said."

We both stood there. Lost in thought.

"Did you know he knits?" I asked Bubba.

Bubba laughed. "Yeah. I went to the library once. Caught him red-handed."

"So did I!" I said with a chuckle.

"I think he could care less who knows," Bubba said.

"A man that size? I guess he figures no one is going to mess with him about it," I quipped.

"I know *I* wouldn't," Bubba said with a hearty laugh.

"Me neither," I said.

"You'd have to be an idiot to bust his chops about it," Bubba said.

"Or blind."

"Yeah," Bubba laughed. "Or insane."

I smiled with the memory. "He tried to teach me to knit."

Bubba laughed. But then he grinned. "Me, too."

"He tried to teach *you*?" I asked, laughing.

Bubba nodded.

"How did you do?" I asked.

"Not so great," Bubba admitted. "You?"

"Don't even ask," I said.

Bubba shrugged. "Henry loves it. Says it relaxes him."

I shook my head. "It was *not* relaxing."

"Yeah," Bubba agreed. "It wasn't my thing either."

"It was frustrating," I added.

"Guess you'll have to find something else to relax you," Bubba said with a grin.

I nodded.

My mind went back to the plans.

"So you know who dropped off that truck? The one the plans were in?" I asked Bubba.

Plans

The smile left Bubba's face.

"It's a sad story," he said.

"You *know* whose truck it is?" I asked.

"You mean, truck it *was*," Bubba said.

I was confused. "What are you talking about?"

"The guy who owned the truck? He's dead."

Oh. Wow. Okay. "I'm so sorry," I said.

Bubba snorted and shook his head. "It was terrible. The war in Iraq didn't kill him. But a stupid accident did. He wasn't wearing his seatbelt. Can you believe that?"

"That's sad," I said.

"Tell me about it," Bubba said. "The woman he was going to marry? She's a mess."

Chapter 11

That poor woman!

How sad.

I guess I'd have to find out what I could on my own.

I didn't want to hurt the man's fiancé. I didn't want to bother her.

She didn't need to hear a bunch of questions.

She didn't need me reminding her.

She had her own grief to deal with.

Her own problems.

"What did he do in Iraq?" I asked Bubba.

"Beats me," he said.

"Hm. I wonder. How can I find out?" I asked myself.

Plans

Bubba answered. "You'll have to find an inside guy."

"An inside guy?" I asked.

"The military probably won't help you."

Bubba was right. I'd have to track this down by myself.

"Any idea on how to start?" I asked Bubba.

He wiped his hands on a rag.

"Hang on. I have a friend. He's in the reserves. He might be able to help you."

Bubba walked to the phone and dialed.

It was across the room.

I couldn't hear him. But I watched him as he spoke with his friend.

I watched as he laughed.

I watched as he joked around.

Then I watched his face turn serious.

I saw tears well up in his eyes.

I watched him nod. I watched him take out a pen and write something down.

Bubba looked over at me.

He gave me a thumbs up.

I knew he'd gotten the name of someone I could speak with.

Good ol' Bubba. He always came through.

I watched as he hung up the phone.

He stuck the pen back in his pocket. The pocket of his black t-shirt.

"Okay," he said. "I got you a number."

"Thanks, Bubba."

"No problem," he said. "I want to find out what those plans are. Same as you."

I nodded.

"Part of me wants to return them to the military. But in case they'll get the guy in trouble? I don't want to turn them in just yet," I said.

"I agree," Bubba said. "Let's find out what it's all about first."

"And why he had them. Why he hid them in his truck door."

"Yeah," Bubba said. "I want to know that too!"

Chapter 12

I drove to the soldier's house.

I rang the doorbell.

He came outside.

He was young. Strong.

He stood tall. Proud. Confident.

"Thank you for meeting with me," I said.

"No problem, sir," he replied.

"Please," I said. "Call me Dan."

"Okay, Dan, sir."

I felt like saying, "At ease, soldier." But I didn't.

"So how may I help you, sir? Dan, sir," he said.

"I have some questions about Mike. Mike Noyes."

"He was a good man, sir," he said.

"Yes," I said. "I know that. I'd like to know about his time in Iraq."

"It was our duty to serve, sir," he replied.

I swore he stood a little taller than before.

Which was hard to believe. The man stood stick straight to begin with.

"It was an honor," he said.

He stood at attention.

"It was also our privilege," he added.

"Yes," I said. "Yes. I'm sure."

"And our job," he stated.

"Yes. And we appreciate all you did, Ramon."

He nodded curtly. "Thank you, sir."

"But I need to find something out," I started.

I looked into his eyes.

They showed nothing.

No softness.

No twinkle.

No answers.

No emotion.

Nothing.

Plans

He did not stare blankly. But he did not reveal anything, either.

He seemed intelligent. Even thoughtful. But he was not giving anything away.

Not his opinion.

Not his emotions.

Nothing.

He didn't offer his help.

But then, he didn't deny it, either.

He seemed to be waiting.

Waiting for me to speak.

"There were plans," I said.

He didn't blink.

"There were many plans, sir," he barked.

"Yes. I'm sure," I said.

I had to approach this carefully.

If I wanted him to help me? I had to let him know one thing.

I wasn't there to hurt him.

Or Mike.

I just wanted info. That's all.

"Did you know of the plans *Mike* brought

back?" I asked.

His face tightened.

His jaw twitched.

But besides that? Nothing.

No show of emotion.

But that tightening—that twitch—said it all.

I waited.

Waited to see if he would respond.

"He did nothing illegal," the soldier said.

"I didn't think he did," I replied softly.

I wanted this man to soften up. To talk to me. To tell me what was on his mind.

What was on *Mike's* mind.

Especially when Mike brought that map home.

The fact that it was hidden meant something.

I had no idea *what* it meant.

But it meant *something*.

And the map had to mean something to Mike.

Or he wouldn't have brought it home.

Chapter 13

"He would have returned it," Ramon finally said.

I saw another twitch.

I knew I'd hit a nerve.

I just wished I knew *why*.

"He was signed up for another tour," he added. "But…"

Another twitch.

"He didn't make it."

I nodded.

"I know," I said gently. "He died in an auto accident."

The soldier looked past me. Or maybe through me. But not *at* me.

"It was a waste of a great soldier," he said.

"It was a waste of a great life," I added.

Ramon turned his head. He tilted it.

Now he looked at me.

I think he was seeing me for the first time.

His eyes softened.

His jaw loosened.

His spine curved. Ever so slightly.

"Mike was a great guy," he said mildly.

Gone was the crisp soldier. Gone was the tightness.

Gone was the attitude.

"Please. Tell me about him," I said calmly.

Ramon looked off. Into the distance.

I let him gather his thoughts.

I let him sift through his memories.

"He was a good man," Ramon said. "Cared about everyone."

I nodded.

"He did his best to make sure we were safe," he said.

"In Iraq?" I asked.

Plans

"Yes, sir," Ramon replied.

"That must have been hard," I said softly.

He nodded. "It was, sir. Very hard. You have no idea!"

He was right. I didn't.

I had no idea what these men went through.

"Tell me," I urged.

He looked at me. Hard. Trying to judge.

Judge if I were worthy.

Worthy enough to share their secrets.

I wasn't one of them. I knew that.

I hadn't been through what they had been through.

I was an outsider.

Sure. I felt for them. Our soldiers.

Sure. I supported them.

I thought they were amazing!

But I hadn't shared what they'd been through.

He paused. Tried to decide.

Should he tell me?

Shouldn't he tell me?

I could see he wondered why I wanted to know.

Finally he spoke.

"You want the truth?" he asked.

"Yes," was all I said.

Chapter 14

He looked at me again.

I wondered if I measured up.

I tried not to droop.

It was hard to stay steady. Confident. Not under his gaze. His stare.

His glare was intense.

It was daunting.

I didn't feel bullied.

I just felt… weak, under his strong glare.

Like a butterfly must feel. Under a microscope.

Or a magnifying glass.

He was examining me.

I wondered how I measured up.

I wondered how he saw me.

Did he see me as strong? Weak?

A team member?

An outsider?

A coward?

I knew how I saw him.

Strong.

Tough.

A hero.

I saw him grimace.

He opened his mouth to speak.

At first, nothing came out.

Then he spoke.

"Man, it was *hell* there!" he said softly.

I was surprised.

I wasn't expecting that.

I didn't know what I was expecting.

But it wasn't that.

I waited.

"Hot as hell," he said.

I nodded. Listening.

"The people didn't want us there," he said.

I stayed still. Silent.

Plans

"The food was hell," he said.

I waited for more.

"There wasn't one nice thing about that place!" he said.

I nodded.

"Nothing!" he said. "It was hell there."

I could picture it in my mind.

Was thankful that I was only picturing it.

Many men and women had to go there. To *be* there.

To *stay* there.

Once again. My heart went out to them.

My heart. My thanks.

My respect.

"But that's not how Mike saw it," Ramon said.

He'd interrupted my thoughts.

It took me a few seconds to realize what he'd said.

"What?" I asked.

"Mike didn't see it as hell."

"No?" I asked.

"No. Mike was different."

He *must* have been.

"How so?" I asked.

Ramon smiled sadly.

"Mike was selfless," he said. "It's hard to explain."

"Try," I urged.

He nodded.

"Mike did things," he said.

"Did things?"

"Yes, sir," he said.

"Like what? What kind of things?" I asked.

"Things like…"

He stopped again. As if he couldn't decide if he should tell me.

I let him make up his mind.

"Mike went out on recon," Ramon said finally.

"Recon?" I asked.

"To gain info. Get the lay of the land."

"Oh. Right," I said.

"Man, *everybody* hated us."

I nodded.

"It was dangerous there. Still is," he said.

Plans

"Yes," I said. "I read about it daily in the newspapers."

He made a face. "You can *read* about it. But it's *far* worse when you're *in* it!"

"I can't even imagine," I said gently. And I meant it, too.

"And they don't even print a *lot* of it," he said tightly.

His jaw stiffened.

"Why don't you tell me," I said gently.

Chapter 15

He sat down on the stoop.

He put his elbows on his knees.

He put his hands on his head.

I sat down next to him.

I touched his shoulder.

Ramon looked at me.

He took a deep breath. He let it out slowly.

"Land mines were everywhere!" he said

I thought of the plans. The map.

The symbols I'd seen.

The ones that Henry said were land mines.

There were a lot of those.

The map was covered with them.

I looked at Ramon.

Plans

He was staring at the ground now.

Focused on a pebble.

Staring at that pebble.

But I don't think he was seeing it.

He was seeing something else.

"Guys in trucks," Ramon said. "Everywhere."

He reached out and touched the pebble.

"Trying to blow us up," he said.

The pebble flew from his fingers.

I watched it arc.

Watched it fly through the air.

Watched it land. And bounce.

Once. Twice. Three times.

It came to a stop.

It hadn't changed. It looked the same.

The same pebble. In a different spot.

A different place.

But still the same pebble.

I looked at Ramon.

In way, he had flown through the air. Like that pebble.

He'd gone to Iraq.

He had landed. Like that pebble.

Only, in Iraq.

He had probably bounced. Like that pebble.

Once. Twice. Three times.

Maybe more.

Like that pebble.

And he had come to a stop. Like that pebble.

Just like that pebble.

The pebble hadn't changed.

But Ramon had.

I watched him. Gave him space. Gave him time.

He sighed loudly.

Then he shook his head.

Then he wiped his hand over his short-cropped hair.

"It was nuts, man!" he whispered.

He looked like he was in pain.

"Kids. *Kids*! They had machine guns," he said. "They should've been playing baseball. Watching cartoons. Doing homework!"

I watched his face as it showed shock.

Plans

"But they were out there. Trying to kill us."

I shook my head. "I can't imagine," I said.

"It's *true*," he said with anger.

"Oh, I don't *doubt* you," I said quickly. "I just can't imagine it."

"It's hard to imagine," he said quietly.

He swiped his hand over his head again. Like he was trying to wipe away the memories. From the outside.

"I was there," he said. "I saw it. Lived it! And I *still* can't imagine it," he whispered.

"I've heard stories. Stories of Vietnam. Similar stories," I told him.

He shook his head.

He rubbed his eyes.

As if by rubbing them, he could remove what he'd seen.

It didn't work.

He obviously couldn't get the pictures out of his head.

I felt sorry for him.

I couldn't imagine what he was thinking.

Feeling.

> I knew it couldn't have been good.
>
> He looked at me.
>
> He didn't stare at me like he did before.
>
> His eyes weren't hard now.
>
> He wasn't judging me.
>
> Just looking at me. Another human being.
>
> His shoulders sank.
>
> He looked sad. Tired.
>
> He finally spoke.
>
> "War sucks, man," he said heavily.
>
> I just nodded.

Chapter 16

He needed time.

Time to compose himself.

I sat next to him while he did.

"I've never said that before," he said quietly.

I put my hand on his shoulder.

"At least, not out loud," he added.

I nodded.

"It must be hard to admit," I said.

"Yes, sir," he said. "It is."

We sat in silence.

Each with our own thoughts.

"You're not the first to think it," I told him.

He shrugged. "Probably not."

"I'm sure you're not the first to *say* it, either," I

said gently.

He looked ashamed.

"It's not shameful," I said. "To admit something like that."

He was silent.

"It's also not a weakness, you know," I told him.

"It's dishonorable," he said.

"It's truthful," I countered.

He sat quietly.

I could hear him breathe.

I squeezed his shoulder.

I didn't know what to say to him. I had no words.

"I have to go back," he said.

I wasn't expecting that.

Again. I didn't know what to say.

We sat in silence.

"I'm sorry," I said.

That's all I could think of to say.

He sat up. Straight.

He took a deep breath.

Plans

Renewed strength coursed through him.

It made him hard. Tough. Like a wall.

The soldier was back.

"Let's talk about something else," he said.

He turned his head. He looked at me.

He smiled briefly.

Then he stood.

His back was straight.

His feet planted.

His legs braced.

"What do you want to know?" he asked.

He was all business now.

"Tell me about those plans," I said.

Chapter 17

"Mike's map?" Ramon asked.

I nodded. "Yes."

He started to laugh. Not a ha-ha, funny laugh. But the laugh of a cynic.

Not really a laugh at all.

Then he shook his head.

"You're not going to believe it," he said.

"Try me," I replied.

"That was Mike's own map," he said.

I listened.

"His personal map," he added.

"So it's not owned by the military?" I asked.

He shook his head.

"No."

Plans

That was great!

It let me off the hook.

I didn't have to worry about it anymore.

"Every night. Under the cover of darkness. Mike went out," Ramon explained.

Sure. I didn't need to hear this. I was done.

Done with my duty.

The plans weren't property of the government. So I was off the hook.

I could go home now.

I could get back to living my life.

But I was curious. "Why?" I asked. "Why did Mike go out?"

"Recon."

I nodded.

He laughed a hallow laugh.

"But Mike took things a step further," he said.

"How?"

He looked around. Like he was worried. Worried that someone was listening.

"He worried about our safety," he whispered.

"So?" I whispered back.

"So he was a very friendly guy," Ramon said softly.

What did *that* mean?!

"He made a friend," Ramon said softly.

"A friend?" I asked.

"Yes, sir," he said softly.

He was still looking around.

"What kind of friend?" I asked.

"Someone who shouldn't have been a friend," Ramon whispered.

I didn't know what to say.

I had no idea what he was talking about.

So I figured I should keep my mouth closed.

"Mike went out at night," Ramon said.

I still didn't get what he was trying to say.

"He made a friend. A friend who told Mike where all the land mines were."

Oh. *Now* I got it.

Mike was consorting with the enemy.

"He told Mike *everything*."

"Like what?" I asked.

"Like where to go. When to go. Places we

Plans

should stay away from."

That would be great advice. Especially when you were in a war zone.

"He told Mike what was about to explode. Where. And when."

"That's some pretty great info," I said.

And it was! Imagine. If you *knew* where your opponent would be. What he was up to.

How and when he was going to strike.

Like I said. That was some pretty great info!

"No kidding," Ramon agreed. "We didn't lose *one* man. Not one!"

"That's amazing!" I said with awe.

"Yes, sir. And we owed it to Mike."

I had to agree. But I also had to add one thing.

"Sounds like you also owed it to Mike's, ah, friend."

Ramon nodded. He face became thoughtful.

"Yes, sir. You're right."

Chapter 18

"So when are you going back? I asked.

"In a couple of weeks," he answered.

His voice held no emotion.

Just stated a fact.

He would go back to that place. That place he referred to as "hell."

Would go back in a couple of weeks.

I felt for him.

I thought about that map.

Now that I knew what some of the symbols were? I could picture the danger.

I could see how one would want a "friend."

Need a "friend."

"Do you know who Mike's 'friend' was?" I

Plans

asked.

Ramon shook his head.

"No, sir."

"Do you think anyone knew?" I asked.

"No, sir. That would have endangered Mike. And the source."

"Source?" I asked.

"The 'friend,'" Ramon explained. "If his people found out? He'd be killed."

I nodded.

"They'd probably make an example of him," Ramon said.

"How?" I asked.

Ramon looked me in the eye.

"His death would not be an easy one."

He wanted to make sure I understood what he was saying.

I understood.

"Torture?" I asked.

"Like you can't imagine," Ramon said softly.

I thought of that "friend."

Of what he'd risked for Mike. For Mike's men.

For *our* men.

He'd risked a lot.

Put himself in grave danger.

For us.

He was… a hero.

We owed him a great deal.

And then I knew.

I knew what that **X** with the **✚** on top was. The star.

At least I *thought* I knew.

"Could that have been where they met?" I asked Ramon.

"Possibly," he said. "It could be where he lives, too."

My mind was racing.

"Or it could be anything," Ramon said. "It was Mike's own map. It could mark the best bathroom, for all we know."

"But you said Mike was selfless," I noted.

Ramon raised his eyebrows. "So?"

"So. If he were selfless? Why would he mark the best bathroom, and not share it with everyone

Plans

else?" I asked.

That made Ramon laugh.

"Because if you shared the best bathroom with hundreds of other guys? It would no longer *be* the best bathroom!" he said with a chuckle.

I had to laugh at that.

I tried to imagine a bathroom shared by hundreds of men.

Not pleasant.

"So nobody knew him? This 'friend' guy?" I asked.

"Nobody but Mike," he said.

"Wasn't anyone curious?" I asked.

"Yes, sir. Lots of people were curious. But we're not stupid. If the 'friend' were exposed? We'd lose our edge."

That was true.

"Have you seen the death toll?" he asked.

Sadly, I had. "Yes," I said simply.

"So you know why no one would want to mess with our source."

"Yes," I said. "I understand."

Elise Leonard

We sat there.

Each thinking our own thoughts.

I didn't know what Ramon was thinking about. But I knew what was on *my* mind.

Mike.

Mike never told anyone about this "friend."

They knew *about* him. But not who he was.

Then I thought of Mike's fiancé.

Yes, my marriage was just about over.

But when it was going on? I liked to tell Patti about good things.

I never told her about bad things.

I tried to protect her from that.

But the good things?

I always wanted to share those.

I thought Mike would be the same way.

After all. When a woman loves you? When you love a woman? You don't want her to worry about you.

You'll do anything to make sure she doesn't worry about you. You'll say anything.

I needed to speak with Mike's fiancé.

Chapter 19

Ramon called her. She said she'd speak with me.

I didn't speak with her. Ramon did. But from what I heard, she sounded nice.

It took a half hour to get there.

I walked up to the house, and knocked on the door.

An older woman came to the door.

"Hello," she said. "You must be Mr. Corbett."

We shook hands.

"Please call me Dan," I said.

A young woman came over to us.

"Hi," she said shyly. "I'm Robin."

"Hi, Robin. I'm Dan. Thanks for seeing me."

She smiled sadly. "No problem. What can I do for you?"

"I'm sorry about Mike," I said softly.

She bit her lower lip. Her eyes started to fill with tears.

She nodded quickly. "Thank you."

"I hear he was a good man," I said.

The tears slid slowly down her cheeks. "Yes. He was."

I didn't know what to say next. So I just said what was on my mind.

"I'm here because we found a map. Mike's map."

Her face lit up. "You found it?" she blurted out.

"Yes," I said. "You knew about it?"

She nodded. "I couldn't find it. After he… died."

She let out a little sob. It sounded like the cry of a small bird.

My heart went out to this young woman.

"Where was it?" she asked. Her voice was small.

Plans

"It was hidden in the door. The door of his truck."

Robin smiled widely.

"Good hiding place," she said.

Then she giggled.

"Mike was great with hiding places. He used to send me on treasure hunts."

"Sounds like fun," I said.

"I didn't know what was more fun. The treasure hunt. Or the small gift at the end."

Her smile was beautiful.

"The gifts were never large. Or expensive. Just thoughtful," she said with a sigh.

"Sounds nice," I said. And I meant that.

"He would put maps and clues all over the place. I'd have to figure out the next place."

I had to smile.

"His poetry was awful," she said.

Then she laughed lightly.

"But he tried," she said.

"We always do, for the women we love," I said gently.

Elise Leonard

That made her cry.

I was so upset.

I didn't want to make her cry.

"I'm so sorry," I said.

Robin wiped at her tears.

"Don't be," she said. "That was a beautiful thing to say."

I just stood there.

"Mike would have said something like that," she said.

I still stood there.

"So what do you want to know? About the map?" she asked.

"You know what it means?" I asked.

"Yes," she said with a smile.

I took out the map. Unrolled it.

"What's this?" I asked.

I pointed to the star.

"That's where the boy lived," she said.

"The boy? You mean Mike's friend was a *boy*?"

She nodded. "Kids understand peace more than

Plans

adults."

I smiled at that.

"Perhaps kids understand *war* more than adults," I said sadly.

She nodded. "Yes. I think so."

She took my hand. "Please come with me. I want to show you something."

She took me inside her house.

Into the living room.

She pointed to a shelf. "See that?"

"Yes."

"That's what Mike was going to bring back. To that star. On that map. The boy."

I looked at the shelf.

It held a portable DVD player. Still in the box.

And a stack of DVDs.

She walked to the shelf. She picked up the DVDs.

She handed them to me.

Rush Hour. Rush Hour 2. Rush Hour 3.

Every Vin Diesel movie ever made. *The Fast and the Furious. The Chronicles of Riddick. The*

Pacifier.

Then there was *Dodgeball: A True Underdog Story.*

Super Troopers.

Anchorman: The Legend of Ron Burgundy.

Ghostbusters 1 and *2*.

Honey I Shrunk the Kids.

Caddyshack.

Austin Powers.

"Those were all for the boy," she said.

I looked at her.

"Mike bought it all. With his own money. To thank the boy," she said.

She took out an mp3 player. "Mike even loaded this up. With cool American songs."

She handed me the mp3 player.

I looked through the index

Hip Hop. Latino. Classic Rock. Country. Rap. Pop. Heavy Metal. You name it. It was on there.

"Great collection," I said.

Robin nodded. "The boy would have loved it."

Then I got an idea.

Chapter 20

"Hey, boss," Bubba called.

He was walking to the office. My office. The junkyard office.

"What now?!" I roared at Bubba.

Bubba waived a paper bag around. He was teasing me with it.

Like one would shake a rattle in front of a baby.

I didn't like it.

"Stop waving that bag around!" I huffed.

"You sure are grumpy," Bubba said.

He was right.

I was behaving badly.

"I'm sorry," I said. "I didn't sleep last night."

"Why not?" Bubba asked.

"I was thinking about Ramon."

"Oh," Bubba said. "Right."

"He should be there by now," I said.

Bubba knew what I was talking about.

I'd told him about Ramon. And Iraq.

And how Ramon felt about the place.

Miles came through the door. "Hey, Dan. Hey, Bubba. Just wanted to let you know—I'm back."

Miles was homeless. He came and went from the junkyard as he pleased.

"Good to have you back," I said.

Bubba waved the bag at Miles. "Guess what's in here?"

Miles looked at me.

I rolled my eyes.

Miles shrugged.

"I'll guess," Miles said. "A ham and cheese sandwich?"

"Nope," Bubba said.

"Too bad," Miles said. "I could use one of those."

Plans

I hitched my thumb behind me. "Go on in the kitchen, Miles," I said. "Make yourself a sandwich."

"Thanks," Miles said. "Don't mind if I do."

"Make me one, too," Bubba said.

"Who said *you* could have one," I said.

Bubba looked hurt. "I can't?"

I grinned. "I'm only kidding. Of *course* you can have a sandwich," I said.

"Want one, Dan?" Miles asked.

I couldn't eat. I was too worried about Ramon.

Just then, I got an email.

Subject: The package is with the star

Dan,

The package is with the star.

The star is shining brightly.

The star is watching over us once more.

The star is… star struck.

Thanks for arranging this.

It was signed, R.

Just "R."

But I knew who it was from.

I also knew who the star was.

I was glad he was happy with Mike's gifts.

I was also glad he was still watching over our soldiers.

This boy—this child—was a hero. *Is* a hero.

I'd added more to Mike's gift.

I wanted to thank the boy myself.

I added a personal video game player. And many games.

I wanted the boy to have some time to be a kid.

I figured kids in war-torn countries don't get to be kids.

I wanted to give him that.

He gave our men and women safety. And life.

I wanted to give him a childhood.

However meager.

I looked at Bubba. "Okay. So what's in the bag?" I asked.

"It's a bag of *money*! I found it stuffed in one of your cars!"

"Oh no," I said. "Here we go again!"

Now that Dan has solved *this* problem, read the next **JUNKYARD DAN** book, **MONEY FOR NOTHING**, to find out about the bag of money they found in that car. Whose money was it? And why didn't anyone report it missing? Didn't they want it?! Find out by reading the *next* book in the series!

And we have a few **other** series that you might like too:

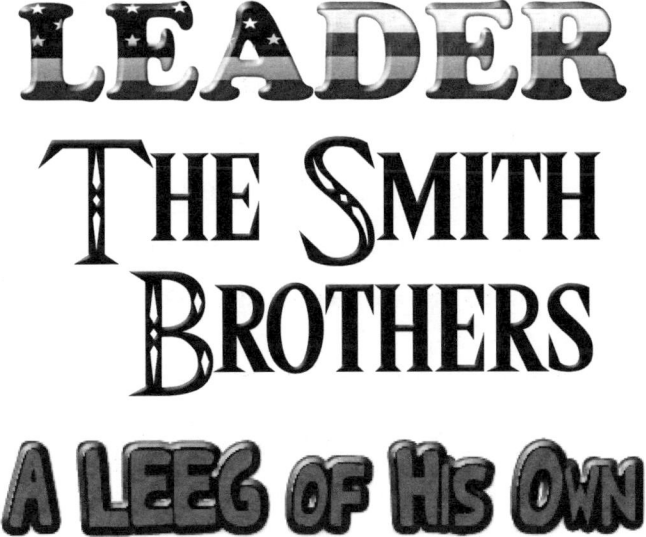

Want to read more NOX PRESS books?

Go online to
www.NoxPress.com
to see what's being released!

Books can easily be purchased online or you can contact **Nox Press** via the Website for quantity discounts.

Are you a fan?

Do you want us to put *your* comments up on our Website?
If so, please e-mail them to:
NoxPress@gmail.com

NOX PRESS
books for that extra kick to give you more power
www.NoxPress.com